A Treasury of
Children's
CLASSICS

Commissioning Editor   Christine Deverell
Additional Illustrations   Richard Deverell
Design   Ian Jones

©2000 Robert Frederick Limited
4-5 North Parade
Bath, U.K.
BA1 1LF

Printed in China

A Treasury of Children's CLASSICS

THREE FAIRY TALES

Adapted by

CHRISTINE DEVERELL

· C O N T E N T S ·

Rapunzel

ILLUSTRATED BY DAVID LONG

Once upon a time there lived a man and his wife who wished for a child, but many years passed, and they were disappointed. From the window of their house they could see a beautiful garden full of flowers and vegetables. It was surrounded by a high wall and no one dared enter there, for it belonged to a Witch whom everyone feared. One day the woman was looking out of her window and saw a bed of beautiful radishes which she longed to eat.

The longing was so great that as the days passed, she became sick for wanting them. Her husband asked her, "Why are you sick?" "I fear that I shall die," she replied softly, "if I do not eat some of those beautiful radishes that I see when I look out of my window." The poor man thought "I do not want my wife to die, so I must get her what she longs for." He waited until it was dark, and climbed over the wall into the Witch's garden. It was quite deserted, and he escaped with a bag full of luscious radishes.

They were such a lovely flavour that the woman wanted more, so the next evening her husband waited until it was dark, and climbed over the wall into the wicked Witch's garden. As he landed on the grass, there was the Witch in front of him.

"You thief! Come to steal some more of my radishes have you? Evil will come upon you for this!" "Please have mercy," begged the man, "I only did this for my wife, for I feared she would die if she did not eat the radishes she saw from her window."

"In that case," said the Witch, "go and help yourself to all the radishes you want, but there will be a price to pay. When you have a child you must give it to me. I will take care of it and treat it as a mother would."

The poor man was so frightened that he consented. A year later his wife gave birth to a baby girl and the Witch gave her the name "Rapunzel" and took her away.

Rapunzel grew to be the most beautiful child under the sun, and when she was twelve years old the Witch locked her up in a tower. This tower stood in the middle of a forest, and had no door, and no stairs. When the Witch wanted to enter the tower, she called up to the window - "Rapunzel! Rapunzel! Let down your hair." Rapunzel had very long and beautiful hair, as fine as spun gold. When she heard the Witch's voice, she opened the window and let her hair fall down to the ground, and the Witch climbed up the hair to the top.

12

Three or four years passed and it happened that the King's son was riding through the forest. As he came close to the tower he heard the sound of a beautiful voice singing, and he looked up to see Rapunzel at her window.

The Prince wanted to reach her, but he saw that the tower had no door. So he went home sorrowful.

Rapunzel's singing had so enchanted the Prince that he rode out to the tower every day just to listen to her. One day he saw the Witch come and call - "Rapunzel! Rapunzel! Let down your hair."

The Prince watched as Rapunzel's hair fell to the ground and the Witch climbed up. "So that is how I must reach her. I will try tomorrow."

So the Prince returned to the tower the next day and when Rapunzel finished singing he called out -

"Rapunzel! Rapunzel! Let down your hair".

Her tresses fell down and the Prince climbed up.

At first Rapunzel was frightened at the sight of a man, for she had never seen one before, but the Prince was so kind and gentle that she soon lost her terror.

He asked her if she would be willing to marry him. The Prince was very handsome, and Rapunzel was longing to be set free from the Witch and her lonely life in the tower.

"I would go with you anywhere but I have no way of climbing down from here. Each time you come to me, bring me silk to weave into a ladder, so I can escape."

The Prince visited Rapunzel every evening because the Witch always came in the day, and they kept their secret safe from the old woman. Then one day Rapunzel said to her, "How is it that you find it so hard to climb up to me, when the King's son is with me in a moment?" The Witch was furious. "I thought I had separated you from the world, and now you have deceived me, you wicked child!" She took a pair of scissors and cut off Rapunzel's beautiful golden hair.

She tied the tresses to the window latch and took poor Rapunzel to a desert where she left her to die. The Witch returned to the tower later that day and waited for the Prince to come. When he called out, "Rapunzel! Rapunzel! Let down your hair." she let down the tresses. He climbed up and into the window, but instead of Rapunzel, he found himself face to face with the Witch.

"Aha!" she exclaimed, "your beautiful bird no longer sits in her nest, singing. The cat has taken her away and will now scratch out your eyes. You will never see Rapunzel again." The Prince was so unhappy that he leapt out of the window of the tower.

He fell into a bush, which saved him from death, but the thorns put out his eyes, and he wandered blind, in the forest.

He wandered like this for two years, until one day, he heard a voice, which he thought he knew, softly singing. As he approached, Rapunzel recognised him and fell on his neck.

Her tears washed over the Prince's eyes and he could see again. Together they travelled to his kingdom where they were greeted with much rejoicing, and where they lived long and happy lives. What became of the old Witch no one ever knew.

The Three Little Pigs

ILLUSTRATED BY KATE DAVIES

O nce upon a time there were three little pigs, and one summer's day they decided to go out into the big, wide world on their own. As they walked along a forest path they talked about what they would do. "We will each need to find a plot and build ourselves a house to live in," said one little pig to his brothers.

They passed a man with a cart piled high with straw. The first little pig asked the man if he could have some straw to build himself a house. The man was glad to give him straw, and the little pig waved goodbye to the other two, built a house and was very pleased with himself. Soon, an old grey wolf came by, and when he saw the straw house he stopped and looked through the window.

23

Inside he saw the little pig. So he went to the door, knocked gently and said, in his sweetest voice, "Little pig, little pig, can I come in?" And the little pig answered, "No, not by the hair of my chinny, chin, chin." "Then I'll huff, and I'll puff, and I'll blow your house down." growled the wolf. And he huffed, and he puffed, and he blew the house down, and ate up the little pig.

Meanwhile the other little pigs walked on, until they met a man carrying a cartload of twigs. One of the little pigs said to the man, "Would you give me some of these twigs to build a house?" And the man was glad to give him the twigs. The little pig waved goodbye to his friend, built a house and was very pleased with himself.

Soon, the old grey wolf came by, and when he saw the twig house he stopped and looked through the window. Inside he saw the second little pig. So he went to the door, knocked gently and said, in his sweetest voice, "Little pig, little pig, can I come in?" And the little pig answered, "No, not by the hair of my chinny, chin, chin." "Then I'll huff, and I'll puff, and I'll blow your house down," growled the wolf. And he huffed, and he puffed, and he blew the house down, and ate up the little pig.

Now the third little pig was much smarter than the other
two. He saw a man with a cartload of bricks, and he thought,
"This is just what I need." So he begged the man to let him have
enough bricks to build himself a house, and the man was happy
to give him as many as he wanted. So the little pig built himself a
fine brick house with a kitchen and a big fireplace. Along came
the wolf who knocked on the door and said, "Little pig, little pig,
can I come in?" And the little pig answered, "No, not by the hair
of my chinny, chin, chin." "Then I'll huff, and I'll puff, and I'll
blow your house down." growled the wolf.

And he huffed, and he puffed, and he huffed, and he puffed, but no matter how hard he huffed and puffed, the wolf could not blow the house down. The little pig laughed at the wolf through the window. The wolf made a plan. "If I want to eat this pig," he said to himself, "then I will have to trick him."

So he called, "Little pig, little pig, I know where there is a lovely field of turnips." "Where?" asked the little pig. "Behind farmer Smith's house; and if you are ready at six o'clock tomorrow morning, I will call for you, and we can go together." "Very well. I will be ready," said the little pig. But the little pig got up at five o'clock, ran to farmer Smith's field, filled a sack with turnips and was safely back in his house when the wolf called for him at six. "Are you ready, little pig?" called the wolf. "Ha, ha!" laughed the pig, "I thought you said to be ready at five. I have already been to the turnip field and now I am making a stew for my dinner."

The wolf was very angry, but in a sweet, gentle voice he said, "Little pig, there is a fine apple orchard at Oakwood Farm. Be ready at five tomorrow and we will go together." "Very well," said the little pig, "I'll see you tomorrow."

But the little pig got up at four and made his own way to the apple orchard. He climbed a tree to fill his sack, and just as he was about to come down, he saw the wolf approaching. The wolf called up to him, "Ah, little pig, you did not wait for me. Are they nice apples?" "Yes, absolutely delicious; I will throw one to you," said the pig. He threw it as far as he could, so that as the wolf ran to catch it, the little pig jumped down from the tree and ran home as fast as he could.

The next day the wolf knocked at the little pig's door and said, "There is a fair in the town this afternoon, will you be going?" "Oh yes," said the little pig excitedly, "I love going to the fair; what time will you be ready?" "At three o'clock," said the wolf. As usual, the little pig left home early and made his way to the fair alone. He bought himself a butter churn, and was on his way home with it when he saw the wolf coming along the road towards him.

He quickly climbed into the butter churn, and set it rolling down the hill and heading straight for the wolf. The wolf was so frightened that he turned tail and ran all the way home again. Later that evening the wolf went to the little pig's house. He stood at the door telling his sad tale of how frightened he had been at the sight of a butter churn coming at him at great speed.

Then the little pig laughed at him and said, "That was me inside the butter churn!" This made the wolf very angry indeed, and he growled, "I will eat you up, I will, I will. I am going to come down the chimney to get you!" As the wolf climbed up onto the roof the little pig stoked up the fire in the huge fireplace, and put a pot of water on to boil.

The wolf fell down the chimney and landed in the pot, and the little pig boiled him up and ate him for supper. The little pig lived safely and happily in his brick house for many years.

The King's New Clothes

ILLUSTRATED BY JAN NESBITT

Many years ago there lived a King who was very rich and liked nothing more than buying new clothes. He did not enjoy hunting, or going to the theatre, except that these occasions gave him the chance to show off his latest outfits. Time passed away merrily in the town where the King had his castle home, and every day people visited his court. One day two men, calling themselves weavers, asked to see the King.

They told him how they knew how to weave materials of the most beautiful colours and patterns, and how the clothes made from these materials were invisible to all who were unfit for the office they held, as well as to those who were exceptionally stupid.

"These must be splendid clothes," thought the King to himself, "and it will be useful to know who in my kingdom is wise, and who is stupid, and who is unfit for the office they hold." "Yes, make me a fine suit of clothes from this fabric," said the King, and he ordered a large sum of money to be given to the two men, so that they might start work at once.

The rogues asked to be supplied with vast quantities of the finest silk and gold thread, which they hid in the cellars of their houses. Then they set up a workshop with two looms, and pretended to work at weaving the amazing cloth.

Everyone in the city heard about the suit of clothes that was being made for the King, and they were all anxious to learn how wise, or indeed how foolish, their neighbours would turn out to be. Not to mention who would be found to be unfit for the office they held.

"I should like to know how the weavers are getting on with my cloth," thought the King one day. But he was a little nervous about going to have a look himself, for he thought it possible that he might be found to be stupid, or unfit to be King.

So he decided to send his faithful old minister, "for he is a man of good sense, and if anyone is fit for his office, it is he," said the King. So the faithful old minister went to see the weavers, and found them working away at the empty looms. "What does this mean?" he said to himself, for he could see no fabric.

"Could it be that I am stupid, or even not fit for my office? I must pretend that I can see it." "Come closer," said one of the knaves, and look at the pattern. Is it not beautiful?" "Yes," replied the old minister, "it is excellent. I will tell his Majesty today just how beautiful it is."

They talked at length about the pattern and the colours, and the minister listened carefully to every word so he could tell the King exactly what it looked like. Then the two men asked for more silk and gold thread to be brought to them, so they could finish making the fabric. They hid these in the cellars of their houses, and continued to pretend to work at the empty looms.

A few days later, the King sent another of his officers to see when the cloth would be ready. When he saw the empty looms he also decided to pretend that he could see the cloth, not wanting anyone to know that he was either stupid, or not fit to hold his profitable office.

So when the two men asked him, "Are you not delighted with the colours and the pattern?" he replied,"Yes, it is very beautiful," and he too listened carefully to their descriptions. He returned to the King with a detailed account of the fabric.

Soon the whole city was talking about the remarkable cloth that was being woven especially for the King. And now the King himself decided to go and examine it.

He selected a number of courtiers to accompany him, including the two who had already admired the cloth.

40

The men appeared to be working hard at the empty looms as the royal party entered the room. The two officers, imagining everyone else could see the fabric on the loom, declared, "Look at these patterns, look at these colours; is it not magnificent?"

"Oh dear," thought the King, "how can this be? I can see nothing. I cannot let anyone think that I am a fool, or that I am unfit to be King." So he said, "It is amazing! I must have a suit of clothes made from this fabric to wear for the procession."

And all his courtiers applauded this decision, even though not one of them could see anything at all.

It was not many days before the grand royal procession was due to take place in the city, and the tricksters sat up late every night, pretending to cut and pin and sew. "Look!" they cried at last, "the King's new clothes are ready."

The courtiers gathered to escort the King to the chamber where the rogues were waiting to dress him in his new suit. As he entered, they raised their arms as if they were holding something up, saying, "Here is your coat, your Majesty," and "Here are your trousers. This is the shirt, and these are the fine undergarments you will need to put on. The whole suit is so light that when you wear it you will feel as though you are wearing nothing at all! "

Not one of the courtiers could see a thing, yet they all declared how exquisite the garments appeared.

"If your Majesty will be pleased to take off your clothes, we will fit your new suit."

The King was undressed by his personal servants and stood in front of a mirror while the two rogues pretended to put on the new suit.

"How splendid his Majesty looks," cried out the courtiers, "and how well the clothes fit,"

"The colours are beautiful," said one, "the design is magnificent,"said another, as the King turned from side to side, admiring himself in the mirror. Out in the streets all the people were talking about the King's amazing new suit. There was great excitement as they took their places, wondering who would be found to be wise and who among them were fools.

Meanwhile, at the palace, the King smoothed down his imaginary coat and his courtiers busied themselves arranging the train on the floor behind him. Then six of them pretended to pick it up and walked proudly behind the King. A crown was placed on his head, and he set off on his grand procession through the streets.

The people gasped as they saw him approach, and cried out, "Your clothes are beautiful!" Not one of them could see a stitch on the King, but they did not want to appear foolish in front of the King or their fellow citizens.

Those who held office, high and low, were mindful of losing their positions in life, so they were not willing to confess to what they really saw.

But there was a little boy in the crowd who had not heard the story about the King's magic suit of clothes, and as the grand procession came into view, the child let out a piercing shriek and cried, "Look at the King! Look at the King! The King has got no clothes on!"

Another voice was heard to say, "The King has got no clothes on!" And then another, and another until the whole town was filled with laughter as they all realised that they had been tricked.

Everyone except the King and his officers was laughing. The poor man walked on in a most dignified manner, with those following holding up the imaginary train until they reached the safety of the palace.

What became of the two tricksters? Well, the instant that the King and his party had left the palace, they raced home, emptied the cellar of their treasure and loaded it onto a cart. By the time the grand procession was over they had escaped into another kingdom, and they lived there in the lap of luxury for the rest of their days.